Fantastic Four
THE SEA MONSTER

by Brent Sudduth
Illustrated by Mangaworx

Meredith® Books
Des Moines, Iowa

Marvel, Fantastic Four: TM & © 2005 Marvel Characters, Inc. All Rights Reserved. www.marvel.com
Licensed by Marvel Characters, Inc.
ISBN 0-696-22509-3 (trade)
ISBN 0-696-22835-1 (kit)

It was a beautiful day at Coney Island Beach, and the Fantastic Four had just arrived to enjoy the hot summer sun! Mr. Fantastic, Invisible Woman, Human Torch, and Thing were ready for a day of fun!

"Last one in the water is a rockhead!" said Human Torch. He rushed by Thing, grabbing his beach hat.

"Hey!" yelled Thing. "You're gettin' a soaking, Matchstick!"

"Ready for some relaxation?" asked Mr. Fantastic, leader of the Fantastic Four.

"More than anything! All I want to do is watch the waves and eat some ice cream," Invisible Woman said smiling.

Invisible Woman began unpacking her beach towel when Mr. Fantastic stretched over to help.

"Please allow me to help," Mr. Fantastic said, smiling sweetly.

"Ahhh, aren't you always the gentleman," Invisible Woman said.

"Can't catch me!" yelled Torch as he held Thing's hat and waved it at him teasingly.

Thing crashed both his fists into the surf, catching Torch in a tidal wave, and down Torch went!

"Very funny," grumbled Torch, soaked to the skin.

"Heh, heh," laughed Thing as he grabbed his hat and made his way back to the others.

Out in the water, played Henry and Bonnie, not paying any attention to the fabulous foursome.

"I am so going to splash you," said Henry.

"Not if I splash you first," said Bonnie.

Henry circled around to get a better angle until he felt something bump against his back.

"Hey, how'd you get behind me?" asked a surprised Henry.

"I'm not, I'm over here," Bonnie said slowly.

Surprised, he turned around to see a large lump in the water.

"What is it?" Bonnie asked.

"Maybe it's a rock," he guessed. Just then, the "rock" opened a gigantic eye!

Invisible Woman saw what was happening and created an invisible force field to separate the beachgoers from the sea monster as it moved toward the shore.

"What is that thing?" asked Invisible Woman.

"There's only one **Thing** on the beach, and that's me!" said Thing. "Hey, Fire Breath, clear a path out to that fish for me."

"I'm on it!" shouted Torch and his body became a fiery figure—the Human Torch! "Flame On!"

The sea monster lurched farther onto the beach, and Thing's eyes widened at the sea monster's massive size.

"Whoa!" said Torch. "It must be forty stories tall!" Torch blasted a path from Ben to the monster, keeping the bystanders away.

Just as Thing was about to grab ahold, the monster's massive tail sprung out of the water and smacked him! Thing skidded across the water like a stone on a pond!

Mr. Fantastic looked up and said, "Torch! I'll take it from down here if you—"

"Take it from up here," Torch finished. Determined, Torch shot a series of fireballs at the monster.

The monster moved so fast that Torch barely knew what hit him. A powerful spout of water came out of the top of the monster's head, snuffing out the fireballs!

Mr. Fantastic stretched his way across the sand and wrapped his super-flexible body around the monster's feet. The monster sent Mr. Fantastic shooting backward like a broken rubber band.

The monster took huge steps toward New York City.

Using her invisible slide to keep up, Invisible Woman saw just where the monster was heading—the Brooklyn Bridge!

"Oh, no!" Invisible Woman cried, "the bridge doesn't stand a chance against this overgrown fish unless I can—"

Concentrating as hard as she could, Invisible Woman used her power of invisibility, and bing—the Brooklyn Bridge disappeared! The monster stopped in confusion . . . the bridge seemed to be gone.

The sea monster turned toward the city as Invisible Woman sighed in relief. "Whew!" Invisible Woman panted, "That was too close!"

"One flying Thing, coming up!" shouted Torch as he carried Thing right over the top of the sea monster's head.

Torch dropped him right onto the back of the monster as Thing yelled, *"IT'S CLOBBERIN' TIME!"*

Thing hurled a mighty fist into the enormous sea monster, and it fell backward, narrowly missing a few buildings.

"Nice going, Rock Head!" Torch teased. "Now I get another shot at this oversized tadpole!"

Torch made a wall of fire that the sea monster quickly turned away from.

"We have it on the run!" said Invisible Woman.

"You're not getting away from me that easily, fish breath!" grumbled Thing. He picked up a bulldozer, and just as he was about to hurl it, the sea monster plucked it out of Thing's hands!

The monster made strange sounds and ran the bulldozer along the street.

"Did it say 'Vroom? Vroom?'" Torch asked, puzzled.

Police sirens rang out, and the monster suddenly dropped the bulldozer and moved toward the sounds. Thing caught the bulldozer just before it hit the street.

"Hey! Where you goin'? We're havin' a fight here!" Thing taunted.

"I've got it!" Mr. Fantastic said. "It likes the sound of the sirens!" Quickly, he stretched his legs as tall as the buildings around him.

"Where's Stretcho goin'?" asked Thing.

"Just get the monster's attention!" ordered Invisible Woman.

Thing picked up a truck and began waving it as Torch threw flames like fireworks around the monster's head.

"Here, boy!" shouted Torch. "Want to be a big, bad fish stick?"

Suddenly, a fire truck arrived, sirens blaring. But as the sea monster reached out for this new toy, it was stopped by something it could not see!

"Mr. Fantastic had better hurry!" said Invisible Woman as she struggled to maintain her force field around the fire truck. **"AAAH-WOOOO-GAAAH!!"** came the loud noise from behind them.

Startled, the sea monster stopped reaching for the truck and began moving toward the new sound, faster and faster.

"AAAH-WOOOO-GAAAH!!"

Mr. Fantastic was holding one of his inventions in the air. It blared out the new sound. "Sounds like Big Brains has its attention!" said Thing, knowing Mr. Fantastic was behind whatever was going on.

Mr. Fantastic soon found himself all the way at Battery Park with the monster quickly following.

"What now?" Torch asked.

"Watch," Mr. Fantastic said mysteriously. The sound blared out again.

"AAAH-WOOOO-GAAAH!!"

Out of the water came another sea monster. This one was *ten times* **BIGGER!** The smaller sea monster raced toward the bigger sea monster and leapt into its arms.

"The sea monster was a kid!" Invisible Woman realized.

"Yes, when it played with the bulldozer and liked the sirens, I guessed it was a kid on the loose," Mr. Fantastic explained. "And we just needed to get junior back to Mom."